CLIMBING
STRONG

BY JAKE MADDOX

text by
Brandon Terrell

STONE ARCH BOOKS
a capstone imprint

Jake Maddox JV Boys books are published by
Stone Arch Books
a Capstone imprint
1710 Roe Crest Drive
North Mankato, Minnesota 56003

www.mycapstone.com

Library of Congress Cataloging-in-Publication Data is available on the
Library of Congress website.

ISBN: 978-1-4965-7524-1 (library hardcover) — 978-1-4965-7529-6 (paperback) —
978-1-4965-7530-2 (ebook PDF)

Summary: Mike Gordon loves a good thrill. And he's not afraid to break the rules to get one.
When Mike goes too far, a friend steers him in the right direction: up. Rock climbing gives
Mike all the excitement he needs. But when Mike faces family troubles, will he fall back into
his old habits?

Editor: Gena Chester
Designer: Sarah Bennett

Photo Credits: Shutterstock: Greg Epperson, Cover, Interior Design Element, rdonar,
Design Element

Printed and bound in China.
000970

TABLE OF CONTENTS

CHAPTER I

IN TROUBLE

Mike Gordon sat in an uncomfortable chair across from Principal Weathers and tried not to make eye contact with her. The thirteen-year-old had been in her office before, had sat in this very chair.

Her stare was legendary at Greenfield Middle School. It forced kids to admit guilt. It made them cry and ask for their parents. It made them vow to never break a single school rule ever again. For these reasons, Mike avoided eye contact.

"Michael," Principal Weathers said. "Look at me. I asked you a question."

Mike slowly raised his gaze from the floor, across the desk, and directly at Principal Weathers.

"Could you repeat the question?" Mike asked.

Principal Weathers's eyes stared daggers at him. "What you did was extremely dangerous."

Mike shrugged. "It was . . . a dare."

What he'd done was earn himself an easy twenty bucks at lunch. Vaughn Underhill, one of Mike's closest friends, had bet him he couldn't climb to the top of the school's flagpole.

Vaughn Underhill had bet wrong.

And it was all going great until the art teacher, Ms. Yang, saw him from her window. She'd walked him to Principal Weathers's office, but Mike already knew the way.

"Peer pressure is a serious thing," Principal Weathers continued. Mike could feel his left leg bouncing. He chewed his fingernails. He needed to get up, to move. "You're a good student, Michael, and you have great potential."

Did he, though? Mike wasn't the type to receive praise. For anything.

Principal Weathers stood. At last, Mike was able to break eye contact. "Your mother will be here any moment," the principal said. "Take the rest of the day and think about your actions. Return tomorrow a better person."

The door to Principal Weathers's office swung wide and Mike's mother breezed in. She looked like she'd fought through an F-5 twister to get there; her dreadlocked hair was coming out of its bun, her shawl was draped loosely on her shoulders, and her eyes looked tired and sad.

"Principal Weathers, I'm so sorry," she said with a sigh. "I got here as soon as I could."

Mike waited in the area outside Principal Weathers's office while the two grown-ups spoke. He couldn't stand still, so he studied the framed photographs on the wall and the trophy case in the corner.

Finally, the office door opened. Mike's mom came out. "Thank you again, Principal Weathers," she said. She walked briskly toward the exit and didn't stop to wait for Mike. He had to run down the empty school hallway to catch up to his mom.

"I did not have time for this today, Mike," she said. She never had time unless it was for Annie.

Mike's sister, Annie, had muscular dystrophy. She had been diagnosed as a toddler. After the diagnosis, the Gordons did everything they could to make sure Annie was taken care of and that she had the same opportunities as her peers. Of course, that meant spending a lot of their time either at her side or working.

The family van was parked in a handicap spot right in front of the school. For a moment, Mike wondered if Annie was in the van. Then he realized that, unlike her older brother, Annie was a good student who was still in her fifth-grade class at the elementary school across town.

"I need to stop at the pharmacy," Mike's mom said as they climbed into the van.

"OK." Mike leaned his head against the passenger side window and watched as Greenfield Middle School receded in the rearview mirror, its flagpole jutting up toward the sky.

* * *

The town of Greenfield was protected on all sides by hills and cliffs. In the hot Utah sun, the whole town felt like it was baking in an oven all summer. It was still spring, though, and the temps were bearable.

Maxwell's Pharmacy was a corner store. A regular at the pharmacy and familiar with its tiny parking lot, Mike's mom was able to successfully navigate the Gordon van into a spot.

As they made their way to the pharmacy counter, past the colorful shelves of aspirin, vitamins, and antacids, Mike saw a familiar face in front of them.

"Why, hello, Sharon. Mike." The tall, muscular man was David Richards. His daughter Hazel went to school with Mike. Hazel and Mike were friends, but mostly school friends. Aside from a few birthday parties when they were younger, the two didn't really hang out.

"Oh, hello, David," Mike's mom said.

Mr. Richards eyed Mike. "How are things? Hope you're not missing school because you're under the weather."

"Mike is fine." His mom waved off the comment. "He's just apparently in the habit of doing ridiculous things to get attention."

"I just climbed the flagpole," Mike blurted out. He didn't know why he felt the need to explain.

Mr. Richards chuckled. "Climbed the flagpole? You've got a bit of a daredevil in you, don't you?"

Mike shrugged.

Mr. Richards glanced at him and said, "Tell you what, Sharon. Maybe Mike would like to join us this Saturday. I know just the thing to help."

Mike opened his mouth to protest. He had plans for Saturday. OK, not really. He was probably just going to hang out with Vaughn and play video games.

"Mike would love that," his mom said. "Besides, we have some appointments at the clinic with Annie. That would be a big help."

"Hazel will be delighted," Mr. Richards said. He clapped Mike on the shoulder. "See you Saturday."

Mr. Richards strolled off toward the checkout. Mike watched him go, then hurried after his mom, who was already moving to the pharmacy counter at the back of the store.

INTRO TO CLIMBING

"Wait . . . I'm gonna do what now?"

Mike tipped his head back, staring up at the cliff face in front of him. It must have been at least fifty feet high.

"You're going to climb that crag," Mr. Richards explained.

"Crag?" Mike asked.

"Rock wall," Mr. Richards clarified.

"Oh. And this is fun?" Mike asked quietly.

It was Saturday morning. The sun hadn't fully risen above the mountains. Hazel and her parents had picked him up before sunrise. It felt weird eating breakfast and leaving the house that early. Mike's dad had been the only other one up, reading the newspaper and drinking a large mug of coffee.

Mike had ridden in the back seat with Hazel. Gear piled up in the way back had clinked and jangled with every bump.

"Here's a harness," Mr. Richards said, handing him some equipment. "I'll show you how to put it on properly. And we'll get you a helmet. The first rule of rock climbing is 'know your equipment and keep yourself safe.' Got it?"

Mike nodded. "Got it."

He couldn't believe it. He was actually going to go rock climbing. Climb actual rocks. Not a flagpole. Or a jungle gym. He stepped into the harness and strapped it tight.

Hazel checked his work. She had her short, dark hair pulled back into a ponytail. She stood close, grabbing his belt and giving it a tug.

"He's ready to go," she told her mom and dad.

Mr. Richards tossed him a helmet. "OK," he said all official-like. "Let's go over the basics."

As the sun and temperature crept higher, Mr. Richards taught Mike about climbing. "It's all about problem-solving," Mr. Richards said. "You need to trust and communicate with your belayer."

"My what?" Mike asked.

"Belayer," Hazel explained. "It's the person on the ground who's securing your rope and making sure you're safe on the crag."

Mr. Richards continued. "Go slowly, especially when you start. Look for hand and footholds that will support your weight."

They followed by rehearsing what would happen once Mike reached the top of the crag, and then he was ready to go.

Hazel walked over and took his rope. It was looped through an anchor at the top that Mrs. Richards had secured when they'd arrived.

"Let's see what you've got," Hazel said. She strapped his rope onto her harness with metal loops called carabiners and wrapped it tight around one hand.

"Wait . . . you're my belayer?" Mike asked.

Hazel nodded. "Sure am."

"Not your dad?" he asked.

Hazel scoffed. "Don't think I can support your weight?" She flexed her right bicep. "Test me, bro."

Mike laughed nervously. He turned to the rock face, reached up, and found a handhold.

At first, climbing was easy. He dug his fingertips into a crevasse in the rock, pulled himself up, and stuck his feet on a ridge. Mrs. Richards climbed beside him, moving slowly and watching him ascend.

"You're doing great!" she said.

He continued up, finding the next handhold, pulling his weight up, securing his feet. Climb, step. Climb, step. Climb, step. He could feel each muscle working, his arms and legs moving as one. His mind started to clear, and all he focused on was the crag in front of him.

It was a wonderful feeling.

When he reached the top, Mike lifted his body over the precipice of the cliff face. Mrs. Richards was already there waiting for him.

"Congratulations," she said. "You completed your first climb."

Mike looked over the edge of the cliff, down fifty feet at Hazel and Mr. Richards. "Great work!" Hazel shouted. Her voice echoed across the canyon. "Now come on down!"

Mike took a look at his surroundings. The mountains were in the distance, the cliffs were around him, and for the first time in a while, he felt at peace.

He calmly slid back over the edge of the cliff and began to descend.

CHAPTER 3

ALONE. AGAIN.

They climbed for the entire morning. Mrs. Richards gave Mike tips on how to belay, and he helped Hazel as she scaled the rock face. Mike marveled at how fast she climbed, but also how smart and sure she was about each movement.

"Been doing it all my life," she said when he complimented her.

"I had no clue." Even though he'd known her for years, not once had the sport of rock climbing come up. It was a pleasant surprise to discover something new about Hazel.

Around noon, they stopped for a small lunch of sandwiches and granola. The cloud-free sky gave them no shade from the sun, and Mike was sweating. But he didn't care; he was enjoying himself.

After a bit of afternoon climbing, they gathered their equipment. Mike told Mr. Richards he felt like he could climb all day.

"You may not feel it now," Mr. Richards said when Mike told him he could keep going, "but you'll be sore tomorrow."

Mike didn't have to wait that long. On the drive back to Greenfield, he could feel his arms and legs stiffen. He picked at a blister that had formed on the palm of his left hand. By the time the SUV swung into the Gordons' empty driveway, Mike's calves burned and his arms felt like Jell-O.

"Thanks again for joining us, Mike," Mrs. Richards said.

"You're welcome anytime," Mr. Richards added. "You've got natural talent."

"Um, thanks," Mike said. He wasn't used to being complimented.

"Hey," Hazel said as he reached for the door. "So there's an indoor climbing wall I visit a couple times a week. It's called King Crag. Any chance you want to . . . I don't know . . . check it out?"

Mike nodded. "Sounds like fun."

"Cool," she replied.

The Gordon van was not parked in its usual spot in the driveway, which meant Mike's parents were still with Annie at her appointment. Mike walked up the ramp his dad had installed by the house's side door, snagged the spare key from atop the security light beside the door, and entered the silent house.

As much as he had enjoyed the peacefulness of the outdoors, the hush of the Gordon house always made Mike anxious. He could feel the jitters returning as he flipped off his shoes in the entryway. His mom had left a note on the table by the door, like always: *Mac & cheese in the fridge. Won't be late. Love you.*

Mike was used to microwaving his dinner. Annie often had doctor's appointments, and more likely than not, both of his parents attended them.

He watched his mac and cheese rotate and pop and bubble in the microwave. When it was done, he set a TV tray next to his dad's recliner, turned on the television, and watched a rerun of an old movie about a group of funny ghost hunters while he ate.

The ghost hunters had just saved the city from a crazy marshmallow creature when Mike saw headlights in his living room window. He heard the garage door outside open. Mike cleaned his dishes up as the door opened and his dad walked in carrying two grocery bags.

"Mike," he said. "Can you help?"

Mike held the door for his mom and sister. His muscles protested and ached. He could barely raise his arm to grab the doorknob.

"Hey, big bro," Annie said from outside as she pressed the controls on her wheelchair forward and ascended the ramp. She sounded tired and Mike couldn't blame her.

"Hey, squirt," Mike replied. "How are you?"

"Oh, you know. Just rollin' along." Annie rolled past Mike. She was followed by their mom, whose arms were also laden with grocery bags.

Mike couldn't wait to tell them all about his day with the Richards family and how it felt to rock climb for the first time. He was sore and exhausted, but man, was he happy.

"What did you do today?" Annie asked him. "And how's Hazel?" Her voice lifted suggestively when she asked the second question.

"What? Ugh." Mike rolled his eyes. "It's not like that. She's fine. We actually went—"

Their mom whisked out of the kitchen, stepping between them and interrupting Mike's story. "Mike, stop bugging your sister," she said. "Annie needs to eat."

"OK, Mom." Annie headed into the dining room. "Come on," she said to Mike. "What's the rest of your story?"

"Never mind," he said. "I'll tell you later."

But they didn't talk later. After Annie and his parents ate—with zero questions about Mike's mac and cheese dinner—they helped his sister to her room and dressed her for bed. Frustrated and no longer wanting to discuss his morning adventure, Mike went to his own room, stuck earbuds into his ears, turned on some music, and flopped down on his bed.

He lay there, not wanting to move, not knowing if he could move, until he drifted off to sleep. As he did, his bedroom door opened and a shaft of light from the hallway was cast across his bed. Mike opened his eyes to see his mom poking her head in. He popped out one of the earbuds.

"How was your day?" she asked. Finally. But Mike was not in the mood to talk.

"Fine," he said, sticking his earbud back in and closing his eyes. The sliver of light from the hallway was swallowed by shadows as his mom closed the door.

Mike was alone.

Again.

CHAPTER 4

KING CRAG

After the final bell rang the following Tuesday, Mike stood on the steps outside Greenfield Middle School and waited. Hazel had texted him, asking if he wanted to go to King Crag. Even though he was still sore from their climb on Saturday, he had immediately responded yes.

Mike picked at the callus on his hand. After his Saturday climb, there was a blister, but now he was ready for more.

"Hey, whatcha lookin' at?" Hazel's voice startled Mike as she exited the front door.

Mike lifted his backpack up on his shoulder and shoved his hands into his pockets. "Nothing," he answered.

"Did you check with your parents?" Hazel asked. "It's OK if we go climbing at King Crag for a while?"

"Yeah, they're cool with it." In fact, Mike hadn't checked with his parents. They probably wouldn't notice anyway.

King Crag was a couple miles from school, so the two buzzed through Greenfield on their bikes. The building was tucked in with several warehouses and factories in an area of town that Mike wasn't familiar with. A sign shaped like a crown made of rocks hung over the front door. They stowed their bikes at a rack and went inside.

"Whoa, this place is crazy," Mike said. "I've never seen anything like it before." The space was filled with gray climbing walls covered in colorful hand and toeholds. Ropes hung from the rafters.

Several climbers were already climbing the walls. One woman was even hanging upside down from an archway cut into one of them, gripping to her handholds while her belayer below shouted encouragement.

"There are more walls in the back," Hazel said, pointing. "And an obstacle wall."

"Hey, Hazel," a young man said as he passed. The teenager was a few years older than them. He wiped his sweaty forehead with a towel.

"Hey, Derek!" Hazel responded over her shoulder as she led Mike to a row of orange lockers. "That's Derek," she explained. "He's in high school and works here part-time. But he's here, like, every day. Derek's one of the best climbers I know."

"Are you a regular?" Mike asked.

Hazel nodded. "My family comes here a lot."

Hazel was an only child. She didn't have to worry about her parents splitting their attention between more than one child. Didn't have to share the spotlight.

From one of the lockers, Hazel produced a pair of harnesses and helmets. It was much easier to strap into the harness than it had been the first time, even though Mike was still sore.

Mike chewed his fingernails and waited while Hazel chose a good starting spot for them. "Here," she said, picking an empty space. "It's more of a beginner course."

"Beginner?" Mike chuckled. "I thought I was an expert now."

"After one day of climbing?" She laughed. "You wish!"

Mike hooked himself to the nearest rope and Hazel got ready to belay.

The rubber hand and toeholds were easy to grasp, and Mike found himself scaling the wall with ease. He reached the top and whizzed back down to the floor.

"See?" he said. "Expert."

Hazel said nothing, but instead led him to the tallest climbing wall at King Crag. It was an enormous 40-foot tall crag.

"OK, expert," she said. "Show me you can tackle The Monster."

"The Monster?" Mike craned his neck to look up at the wall. "Why is it called The Monster?"

As if in response, a climber who was halfway up the wall suddenly lurched upward, reached for a handhold, and missed. She fell, caught in mid-air by her belayer. The dangling woman yelled in frustration.

"Even the best climbers struggle on The Monster," Hazel said. "You wanna give it a shot?"

"Sure," Mike said excitedly.

Mike latched himself to the rope, and Hazel prepared to belay for him. Hand over hand, feet sliding up until they found a toehold, Mike stepped and reached. He kept his eyes up, thinking of nothing but the peak. At numerous points, he found himself grabbing onto a handhold with both hands or a toehold with both feet.

Mike was about halfway up when he realized he was out of his league.

From the ground, the holds were closer together and easy to find. But at twenty-five feet up, they started to move away from one another.

Mike reached for the nearest hold and found he couldn't even touch it with his fingers.

I have to jump.

He made the mistake of looking back down at Hazel on the ground. Derek now stood beside her, watching.

Mike glanced around and saw that Hazel and Derek weren't the only ones watching. A few other climbers had turned their attention to the new guy stuck on The Monster.

He didn't want to jump. Didn't want to fall. But it was his only choice.

Mike crouched as low as he could, took a deep breath . . .

And leapt.

His stomach smacked against the wall, followed by his chin and both arms. His hands slapped the fake stone nowhere near the hold, and he sailed out into thin air.

He fell about five feet and jerked to a sudden stop.

Mike hung his head as Hazel slowly lowered him down. His hands stung, and he could feel the scrape on his chin start to throb.

When he was back down on the ground, Derek said, "You were looking good, new guy. But you lost your focus and stopped trusting your partner." He clapped Mike on the shoulder. "Still, good climb."

As he watched Derek walk away, Mike muttered, "What is that supposed to mean? Stopped trusting my partner?"

"You didn't fully commit to your move," Hazel explained. "You were afraid I wasn't going to be able to catch you."

Mike realized Hazel and Derek were right. But Mike didn't trust most people. It was hard to trust someone when he spent so much time by himself.

"I'm done for the day." Mike unhooked his harness and slipped it off.

"OK," Hazel said. "Mind if I stick around?"

Mike shook his head. "Nah, that's cool."

He dropped the harness in Hazel's locker and headed for the door. As he reached it, a bulletin board on the wall caught his attention. A number of wanted ads were pinned to the board, along with requests for equipment and lessons. A bright red flyer stood out in the middle.

KING CRAG'S ULTIMATE INDOOR COMPETITION! the flyer read. Below it, a pad of entry forms was stuck to the bulletin board. It looked as if some forms had already been torn off.

Mike looked back at Hazel, who was navigating a wall with Derek's assistance. She moved gracefully, not looking down, not worrying about the world around her.

Mike tore one of the entry forms from the pad and shoved it into his pocket.

CHAPTER 5

TO COMPETE OR NOT TO COMPETE

Every muscle ached, but Mike still had homework to finish before bed.

He sat in his room with a science textbook open on the desk in front of him and an ice pack on his right knee. While he hadn't tried his luck at The Monster again, he had spent time on a more advanced wall than the first one he'd climbed.

And he was paying the price for it.

The indoor competition entry form sat on top of the textbook. Instead of reading about chemical reactions, he was filling out his information. At the bottom, there was a spot for a parent's signature. He'd use a pen later to scribble his dad's name in cursive.

"Can I come in?" Annie sat in the widened door frame.

"Sure thing, squirt," Mike said.

"No, really," she said. "Can I? Seems pretty impossible."

Mike looked at his bedroom floor. It was littered with clothes, *Ninja Mummy* comics, and video game controllers. Not exactly wheelchair-friendly.

"Oh," Mike said. "Sorry."

He stood quickly. The ice pack slid off his leg and onto the floor with a thunk. He hoped that Annie hadn't seen it. Wincing, Mike scooped his stuff off the floor and kicked clothes under his bed until there was a clear path for Annie's wheelchair.

Annie wheeled into his room, moving smoothly until she was next to his desk. Mike plopped back down in his chair. He tried to sneakily kick the ice pack into the shadows.

"What's with the ice pack?" Annie asked.

"Nothing, Nancy Drew," Mike replied.

"Uh-huh," she said. "Did you hurt yourself doing something stupid?"

"No." He paused. "It wasn't stupid."

"Does it have something to do with this?" She reached out with her right hand, using all her strength to point at the entry form he'd left in the middle of the desk. Her strength never failed to amaze Mike. Here he was complaining about aching muscles when Annie's constantly ached.

"That?" He tried to sound nonchalant. "That's nothing." Mike opened his top drawer and slid the form into it before she could read it further.

"You're rock climbing now?" Annie asked.

Mike shrugged. "Kinda. Hazel's family took me, and Hazel and I have been visiting this place called King Crag."

"What do Mom and Dad think?" she asked.

Mike tried to keep from laughing. "Mom and Dad? Oh, they haven't asked about it at all."

"Really?" Annie raised her eyebrows.

"Are you kidding me? You know they barely pay attention to me. They're too focused on their little princess," Mike replied.

He didn't mean it to come out that harsh. He was tired and sore and wasn't thinking straight. Still, he could see the hurt in Annie's eyes and immediately apologized.

"It's . . . it's OK," she said. "So what's boring you tonight?" She peered at his homework. "Ooh! Science. Fun!"

"Of course you'd think that." Annie was in the top of her class at school. "We're learning about chemical equations."

"Really? Well, did you hear about the time oxygen went on a date with potassium?" Annie smiled, waiting for her brother to answer.

Mike was confused. "What?"

"It went OK."

Annie burst into a fit of laughter, but it took Mike a minute to realize the atomic symbols of the two elements were O and K. He groaned. "That's terrible," he said, lowering his head onto his textbook with a clunk.

"Oh, come on, you love me," Annie said, still laughing.

"Sure do, squirt," Mike said without raising his head.

Annie stuck around and helped Mike with his homework. And yeah, he tried as hard as he could to focus on the periodic table. But his mind kept returning the entry form tucked away in his desk drawer.

CHAPTER 6

THE SECRET IS OUT

The invitation to the Richards's BBQ party came in the mail two days later. Mike's parents were surprised. They had probably forgotten about the day Mike spent with the Richardses. They certainly didn't know that Mike was spending pretty much every afternoon at King Crag with Hazel. Still, they agreed to go.

So that Saturday, Mike's family drove to Hazel's house. The Richardses lived in a neighborhood of Greenfield where the streets were lined with tall trees and one-story houses.

A few cars were parked on the street in front of their house. Mike's dad pulled the van into the driveway and helped Annie down the platform that extended off the sliding side door.

The sidewalk that led to the Richards's backyard—where Mike could hear music and laughter—wasn't wide enough for Annie's wheelchair. It took an extra push from Mrs. Gordon to get her around to the back.

A smile spread across Mr. Richards's face when he saw them enter the backyard. "Welcome!" He took the Jell-O from Mike and put it on the table alongside bowls of potato salad and chips. When the scent of hamburgers on the grill hit Mike's nostrils, his stomach howled like a werewolf at a full moon.

"My, how you've grown, Annie." Mrs. Richards slid in beside her husband, greeting Mike's family. Hazel was across the yard, tossing a football around with some younger kids.

While their parents stood around and chatted—school and doctors and the same checklist of topics Mike's parents always talked about in public—Mike walked over to Hazel.

"Heads up!" Hazel fired the football at one of the boys, striking him in the chest. He fell to the grass, laughing. The other kids pounced on him.

Hazel brought Mike into the house to show him around. A huge collage of framed photos covered a whole wall in the Richards's living room. Rock climbing. Biking. Whitewater rafting. In each photo, the three of them were a triangle of joy. Father, mother, and only daughter.

"Man, you guys do everything together," Mike said.

"Yeah, kind of," Hazel said. "Want to see my room?"

Mike shrugged.

Hazel's bedroom was very clean, the exact opposite of Mike's. Her bed was made.

A mountain bike leaned against one wall. A bookcase filled with travel guides and journals accompanied a shelf filled with trophies and medals. Mike peered closer at them. Many of the trophies had a little rock climber on them; one was for last year's King Crag competition. Third place.

"Whoa," Mike said. "You didn't tell me you got third last year."

Hazel did her best impression of Mike. "What can I say? I'm an expert."

"Low blow, Richards," Mike said, laughing.

As the two returned to the backyard, Mike noticed right away that his parents were looking at him strangely. His first reaction was to deny whatever trouble they thought he'd gotten into.

But then his dad smiled and said, "Rock climbing?" and it all clicked.

"Is it true?" Mike's mom asked. "Mr. Richards says you've been rock climbing with Hazel."

"And he's quite good," Mr. Richards said.

"When we all went out, it was hard to tell that Mike was a beginner," he continued.

"Really?" Mike's dad actually sounded impressed.

Mike shrugged but said nothing.

"You know," Mrs. Richards said, "David and Hazel were planning on going climbing again tomorrow morning. Would you and Michael care to join them, William?"

"Yes!" Mike's dad said. "I think that would be great!"

Mike looked up at his dad. "Really?"

"Wonderful!" Mr. Richards held up his cup. "Tomorrow it is! Now, who wants a hamburger?!"

CHAPTER 7

A MOMENT OF DISTRACTION

"Hoo boy, that's a lot of information," Mike's dad said. "But I think I've got it. Now if only the coffee would kick in."

It was the following morning, and the foursome was standing alongside the same crag Hazel's parents had brought Mike to on his first outing. The sun's orange glow was just starting to brighten the day.

Mr. Richards had already free-climbed to the top of the crag and had driven a piton into the rock face. The rope dangled in front of them.

Without a word, Mike tied his rope to the harness and used metal carabiners to snap it into place. "Wow," his dad said. "You did that awfully quick. Sure you got it right?"

Mike stared at him. "Um, yeah," he said.

"All right," Mr. Richards said. "Would you like to belay, William?"

"That's the guy holding the rope, right?" Mike's dad asked.

"It is," Mr. Richards replied.

"Gotcha," said Mike's dad. "Then I'm on my way to belay!"

Hazel snickered at Mike's dad's goofy attempt at rhyming. Mike didn't find it funny. In fact, the whole thing was weird. He'd never seen his dad in athletic clothes before, and the old sneakers on his feet must have been about thirty years old.

Mike tried not to think about his dad holding the rope that kept him safe. He cracked his knuckles and began to climb.

Mike found a thin horizontal crack in the stone for his first handhold, but he felt off. He wasn't focused. Still, he pulled himself upward. He was intent on impressing his dad. Though he couldn't decide why this was important. Maybe it was because his dad was actually forced to watch him.

When Mike reached a safe spot, he briefly glanced down and saw his dad staring off into the distance. Then he squeezed his eyes shut and shook his head as if to clear it of cobwebs.

Anger coursed through Mike's veins. *Unbelievable!* he thought. *Of course he's not looking.*

Mike turned back to his climb, but he wasn't thinking straight. He dug his fingers into the next handhold until he felt dirt dig under his nails. To find a safe foothold, he had to spread his legs apart. He spied another ridge above and reached for it.

He was an inch short.

Mike's fingers scraped against the rock. He fell backward, clawing but finding nothing to grab.

Hazel gasped as Mike toppled off the wall.

"William!" Mr. Richards jolted Mike's dad to attention. Mike felt the rope pull taut, felt the snap around his waist and the tightening of his harness. He twisted in midair. The abrupt jerk altered his course and sent him right into the cliff face. He held out his left hand to try and stop his body from hitting the rock wall.

Wham!

Pain erupted through his fingers and palm. His wrist bent back as it was squished between the crag and Mike's body. Mike cried out in pain.

Mike clutched his left hand to his chest as the two dads quickly lowered him to the ground. The moment his feet touched, Mike was using his good hand to unbuckle his harness.

The others crowded around him. "Mike, are you OK?" Hazel asked.

"Fine," Mike replied. It felt like tiny daggers were jabbing his hand.

"Can I see it?" Mr. Richards held out his own hand, palm up. Mike delicately placed his hand atop it. Mr. Richards gave it a thorough look. "Seems to be OK," he said. "Make a fist for me."

Mike did. A sharp intake of air hissed through his teeth.

"I don't think it's a break," Mr. Richards said. "But we should bandage up that cut on your palm. I have a first aid kit in my car."

Through it all, Mike's dad remained silent. He looked terrified. Finally, he spoke. "I'm so sorry," he said. "I don't know what to say. Between work and your sister, I've just been having trouble sleeping. I hope you—"

"Just stop!" Mike waved his dad away and kept walking. "Go back to not paying attention to me. At least then I wasn't getting hurt." *In more ways than one*, he added to himself.

He turned to follow Mr. Richards to the first aid kit.

CHAPTER 8

THE WRONG MOVE

The car ride home was silent.

When the Richardses dropped Mike and his dad off in the driveway, Hazel took Mike's injured hand in hers and quietly said, "It's going to be OK."

He wished he could believe her.

Instead, he walked into the house ahead of his dad, ran up to his room, and slammed the door closed. The entry form for the King Crag Ultimate Indoor Competition was still hidden in his desk. He hadn't turned it in yet. And now, he wouldn't need to.

Mike snatched the form up with his good hand, crumpled it up, and threw it in the wastebasket next to the desk.

* * *

Hazel was waiting for him at the bike rack outside school when he rode up on Monday morning. She'd texted him the night before—*HAND OK?*—but he hadn't replied. It still hurt, but it wasn't broken, just bruised. A ring of purple bruises circled his wrist.

"How are you doing?" Hazel asked as Mike locked up his bike.

He shrugged. "All right."

"Cool. It'll probably be sore when the competition rolls around, but you can fight through it," Hazel said.

"Don't need to worry about that," Mike told her. He walked up the school's front steps.

"What does that mean?" Hazel hurried to catch up.

"I'm not competing," he said.

"Why not?" Hazel grabbed him by the shoulder and forced him to stop just inside the door. Around them, students walked through the halls. The school was humming with activity.

"Because I don't want to, all right?" Mike nudged her hand off his shoulder. The first bell split through the hall, making the kids around them move faster. "I have to go," Mike said, leaving Hazel standing in the middle of the mass of students.

* * *

Mike's gym clothes were in desperate need of a wash. He adjusted his wrinkly shirt, trying to hide the dirt stain as he walked into the gym with the other boys. The usual class—boys and girls both—had been split. The girls stood together on the far side of the gym. Mike squeezed his hand shut, opened it, shut it again. Because he wasn't sure what sort of activity Mr. Hassel had in store for them, he'd wrapped it in gauze. Luckily the bandage was holding.

"Everyone line up!" Mr. Hassel always made the kids line up and answer him with a "Yes sir!" like they were in the military and not Greenfield Middle School's gymnasium. Mike stood on the in-bound line for the basketball court. The rest of the boys hurried to do the same.

Vaughn Underhill ran into the gym, late as usual. Vaughn was tall and lanky, with the start of a mustache. He and Mike had been pals for as long as Mike could remember. As he slipped in beside Mike, he accidentally smacked Mike's bad hand.

"Ouch!" Mike said.

Vaughn noticed, but didn't apologize. "What'd you do?" he asked instead.

Mike didn't answer.

Mr. Hassel counted the boys off and split them into teams for basketball. With a squeak of sneakers, the boys began to run around the court, trying to get open.

Mike didn't want to injure his wrist more, so he didn't draw attention to himself. Unfortunately, Vaughn, playing for the opposing team, tracked him down.

"Hey, I still owe you twenty bucks for climbing the flagpole," Vaughn joked as he crouched in a defensive stance.

"Keep it," Mike said.

"I hear you've been hanging out with that girl a lot," Vaughn said. "Too good to hang out with me anymore? Is she your girlfriend now or something?"

"Knock it off, Vaughn," Mike said.

"Hey, toss it to Gordon!" Vaughn shouted. "He's open!"

Reggie Peterson bounce-passed the ball to him. Mike caught it with both hands. His left palm stung. Vaughn quickly slapped at the ball, but it wasn't the ball he hit. It was Mike's hand.

Mike cried out in pain, dropping the basketball. Vaughn scooped it up and dribbled to the far end of the court, making an easy layup. "Two points!" he said.

With a burst of speed, Mike dashed down the court, heading right for Vaughn. "The play's over, Gordon!" Mr. Hassel shouted. But Mike didn't stop. He barreled into Vaughn. The two fell hard to the floor.

"Hey!" Vaughn struggled to free himself from Mike's grip. "What . . . are . . . you . . . doing?!"

Mike didn't respond, but he did let the anger and frustration of the past few weeks wash over him. Mr. Hassel finally peeled the boys apart.

"Principal Weathers's office," he barked. "Now."

* * *

Mike didn't avoid the icy-blue stare of Principal Weathers this time. He looked her right in the eye.

"Back again," she said. "It seems like you didn't take my words to heart, did you?"

"I guess not," Mike replied.

He and Vaughn sat side by side. Vaughn fiddled with the drawstring on his shorts. Mike's knee bounced, his energy wound tight again.

"Mike and I were just goofing off," Vaughn said. He was not making eye contact with her.

"You call fighting in gym class 'goofing off?'" Principal Weathers asked.

Vaughn paused before answering, "Yes?"

"What do you have to say to that, Mr. Gordon?" She bored holes into him with her gaze.

"Yeah," Mike said. "We were goofing off. It went too far."

Principal Weathers sighed. "I cannot let this go unpunished," she said. "A week of detention for both of you."

The boys stood and began to walk out.

"Mr. Gordon," Principal Weathers called after them. "A moment."

Mike paused in the doorway. Vaughn glanced at him with a 'no man left behind' look.

"It's cool," Mike whispered. Vaughn turned and walked out, leaving Mike alone with Principal Weathers.

"The last time we met," Principal Weathers said. "I asked you to return to school a better person. To use your potential in a positive way." She paused. "This? This is the exact opposite."

"I'm sorry, Principal Weathers," Mike said quietly.

"I know you feel like in order to be seen you have to act like this," she continued. "But you don't. Life is an uphill battle. But when you reach the top? The view is amazing. So keep climbing. It's worth it. You're worth it."

"Thank you." Mike could feel a lump forming in his throat. Tears stung the edges of his eyes. He hurried out of Principal Weathers's office before she noticed.

CHAPTER 9

HEART TO HEART

His parents were going to ground him.

He expected it, of course. He knew that when Principal Weathers called to tell them he would be hanging out in detention for 'goofing off' in gym class, Mike's dad would order him straight up to his room.

"And you'll remain there every night until your detention is over," he would probably say.

So that was why, at the end of the school day, Mike didn't go home. Not yet. Instead he biked to King Crag with Principal Weathers's parting words echoing in his mind.

Keep climbing.

Had she known he'd been rock climbing with Hazel? Or was it just a coincidence? Either way, the words had sparked in Mike a new desire to keep trying. To push himself. To not give up.

And that started with signing up for the King Crag competition.

His entry form was gone, tossed in the trash. He would have to get a new one from the bulletin board.

King Crag was mostly empty; it usually was on weekday afternoons. Mike went over to the bulletin board, and his heart sank. The flyer and forms were gone.

"No!" Mike pounded the wall beside the board with his good hand.

"Hey man, you OK?" Derek stood behind him, looking concerned.

Mike nodded. "I just—I need a new entry form."

Derek's ever-present smile faltered. "Oh," he said. "Well, there are no more forms. The deadline to sign up was today."

Mike's stomach fell, and there was no belayer to catch it. *No more forms?* he thought. *I literally threw away my only shot at competing.*

"There's always next year," Derek said, reading the crushed expression on Mike's face.

"Yeah. OK."

Mike could no longer hear Principal Weathers in his head; now, it was just Derek's voice when he told him the forms were gone. His chances were gone.

Head down, Mike opened the door of King Crag and walked out—and slammed right into someone.

"Whoa there," the person said. Mike's pulse rocketed.

Mike's dad stood before him, arms up, palms out. "I come in peace," he said, smiling.

Mike didn't smile back. "What are you doing here?" he asked.

"Looking for you, actually," his dad said. "Why don't we have a seat?"

There was a seating area with round tables near the lockers and vending machines. Mike and his dad sat at one of the tables. They watched a few climbers traverse the rock walls for a while.

Finally, his dad spoke. "Principal Weathers says you got into a fight."

"Vaughn and I . . ." Mike trailed off. "It was dumb. I let him get under my skin."

His dad nodded. More silence. Then: "You remember when we got the van? How with all the extra features for the platform, the manual was so thick it barely fit in the glove compartment?"

Mike had no idea where his dad was going with this story.

"Well, when you have a kid, there's no manual. Sure, there are loads of books with suggestions and tips. But there's no 'push this button to make them love you' or 'flip this switch, and they'll be brilliant.' When you have that first kid . . . man oh man, it's like you're carrying a work of art, and you're so scared you're going to break it." His dad paused and looked directly at Mike.

"But you? Mikey, I never worried about you. You were fearless. I caught you climbing out of your crib when you were seven months old. Seven months. Nearly gave your mom a heart attack," Mike's dad said.

Mike laughed. He'd never heard that story.

"And when you'd climb to the top of the jungle gym? The other parents at the park were terrified. But not me." He glanced around King Crag. "Come to think of it, I probably should have realized earlier this would be a good fit for you."

Mike's dad swallowed hard and briefly bit his bottom lip. "Then Annie came along. When she got sick, life changed. And she needs us in her corner to help her fight. But you? I never once doubted you'd be safe. And I know it seems like you're alone. I'm sorry it feels that way." He took Mike's injured left hand in both of his. "Even though I may not always be looking, I will always see you. OK, kiddo?"

Mike wiped tears away with his free hand and nodded.

"I'm really sorry about your hand. It's not going to affect the competition, is it?" his dad asked.

"How do you know about that?" Mike responded.

"Your sister told me." He looked worried.

"My hand's fine," Mike said. "Not that it matters. Forms are due tonight, and they're all gone."

Mike's dad reached into his jacket pocket and pulled something out. It was a familiar piece of paper crumpled up in a ball. "Forms like this?"

His dad smoothed the paper out on the table. Sure enough, it was the form Mike had thrown away. The pain and anger weighing Mike down lifted. He wasn't out of the competition, after all.

"You dug through my trash?" Mike asked.

"Again, Annie. Your little sister is a big snoop, isn't she?" His dad grinned.

Mike laughed.

"We'll talk about that fake signature of mine later," his dad said, eyes narrowing.

"Oh. Right." Mike shifted uneasily.

"I added an authentic one, too." Mike's dad shooed him away. "Now go. Turn that thing in and get back on that wall."

"Thanks, Dad. I love you," said Mike.

"Love you too, kiddo," his dad replied.

Mike stood up so fast he nearly knocked over his chair. Then he darted off to find Derek and enter the King Crag Ultimate Indoor Competition.

CHAPTER 10

LET THE COMPETITION BEGIN

The morning of the competition, King Crag had been transformed. Mike hardly recognized the place. First, it was packed with competitors and spectators. Next, there were signs everywhere. They pointed to things like the concession area, restrooms, judges' table, and—

"Isolation room?" Saying it out loud made Mike's anxiety skyrocket.

Hazel, whose parents had given Mike a ride to King Crag, followed his gaze and laughed.

"I'll explain it to you in a bit," Hazel said.

Everyone around him looked like professional climbers. They wore special shoes and T-shirts with names of other competitions on them. Hazel had her hair pulled back by a thick sweatband with the logo from last year's King Crag competition on it. It was almost like they were all marking their territories. Which made Mike's plain white T-shirt really stand out.

Hazel had given Mike some of the rules in the SUV. "It's a speed climbing competition," she'd explained. "That means each climber will be timed. Obviously. But there are also specific handholds we have to use, each numbered as part of the course. They have points associated with them, and our final scores will be accumulated from the number of handholds we reach. Got it?"

Mike had nodded. But now, standing among the group of climbers, there was still a huge part of him that had no clue what to expect.

They reached an open area near the climbing walls that had been sectioned off with velvet ropes. A number of non-climbers stood inside it. "Only climbers are allowed beyond this point," Mr. Richards said.

"We'll keep our eyes out for your family," Mrs. Richards told Mike.

"Thanks," Mike said.

"Good luck," Hazel's parents said at the same time.

Mike and Hazel continued past the ropes.

"Let's sign in and pick up a map," Hazel said. She took Mike's left hand and pulled him in the right direction. He hissed and jerked it from her grasp.

"Wait." She stopped. "Are you still hurt?"

Mike looked around, trying to not be overheard. "Kind of," he said. "The cut and the bruises are gone, but it still hurts when I put too much pressure on it."

"Oh." Hazel looked beyond Mike to the wall. "You think it's strong enough to face that?"

He turned and saw that the climbing wall being used for the competition was The Monster.

"Oh no." Mike rubbed his chin and tried not to think of the last time he'd climbed—*tried to* climb—The Monster.

Derek was near the sign-in table. He flashed them a smile and a good luck. Even though he worked at King Crag, he was still allowed to compete. Like all of the other competitors, Derek wore a tag on his shirt with a number on it.

"Names, please," said a woman behind the table. After checking them off the list, she handed them each a number like Derek's and a route map. "Head on over to the isolation room. We'll call you out one by one for your individual climbs."

Hazel led them to a room behind the concession area where the rest of the climbers were hanging out. Some stood, many sat in folding chairs. Almost all of them were studying their maps. A table had been pushed against one wall. It was filled with granola snacks and bottles of water.

Mike unfolded his map. It was a layout of The Monster with certain handholds numbered one to fifty.

"You have to hit each of those handholds on the way up," Hazel explained. "They'll be easy to see. They're the white ones." She pointed at the large hold with the number one on it. "This one will have tape around it. You have to grab that one with both hands before starting."

"Got it." It felt like a lot of rules, when all he really wanted to do was climb.

One by one, the competitors were led from the isolation room to the climbing area. Each time, Mike could hear the crowd noise swell with applause. "Why are we stuck in here?" he asked Hazel. "I want to watch the others climb."

Hazel shook her head. "Can't. The judges won't allow competitors sizing up the course beforehand. Just one of the rules."

The door swung open. The woman from the sign-in table stood there. "Hazel Richards?" she called out.

"Yo!" Hazel raised her hand.

The woman motioned for her. "You're up."

Mike gave Hazel a high five. "You're gonna crush it," he told her. "Good luck."

"Thanks," she responded.

Hazel stepped out of the isolation room, and the crowed started cheering. Mike began to pace. Back and forth. Back and forth. Chewing on his nails, bouncing on his toes. He felt trapped. It was like being stuck in Principal Weathers's office. Only, he'd take the icy glare of one person over the stares of about thirty.

The door opened, and the woman stepped in again. "Michael Gordon?"

Mike raised his hand. "Over here."

"You know the drill." She nodded at the door.

All right, Mike thought. *Here we go.*

CHAPTER 11

TO COME THIS FAR

Mike took a deep breath and stepped out of the isolation room.

The crowd behind the ropes had grown since he was out there last. They burst into applause when Mike reached the climbing area. It felt odd, being noticed and watched by this many eyes.

"Go Mike!" Annie's voice cut through the crowd. Mike looked over to see his sister sitting right in front at the rope's edge. His parents crouched beside her, nervous smiles on their faces.

He gave them a thumbs-up.

Another section of onlookers had been set up to the right. This one held the climbers, Hazel included, who had already competed. They watched the other climbers with interest.

"All right," said a man in a tracksuit with a stopwatch around his neck. He spoke fast. "You get three shots at the course. Your fastest climb is the one that'll count. Fall all three times and you're eliminated. Got it?"

Mike nodded.

The man grabbed his stopwatch. "Time starts the moment your feet leave the ground. Good luck."

The crowd noise swelled as Mike approached the wall. Then it quickly died away, leaving silence. For the competition, climbers were using an auto belay system. They were attached up above and allowed for safe climbing without a second person. He'd seen people using them before but had not actually tested one himself.

Mike strapped himself in, looked at the white handholds, and did his best to imagine the map. As Hazel had said, the first hold was boxed in with pink tape.

Mike grabbed it with both hands and pulled himself up.

The second his feet were off the ground, the crowd began to cheer. Mike shut it out of his mind. He tried to focus on the wall and not think about how far he'd come since he was in Principal Weathers's office getting punished for climbing the flagpole.

Mike moved smooth and quick, hitting each of the handholds in turn. Each muscle strained but worked together with the rest, like a machine. He wasn't thinking, just reacting to the wall.

Reach, pull, stop. Reach, pull, stop.

Of course, just when he found his rhythm, Mike reached the place where he'd have to leave the wall in order to keep climbing.

The last time he'd attempted this part of the wall, he'd failed miserably.

Phantom pain tingled in his chin. But he refused to spend more time worrying about it. He was being timed, after all. And second guessing himself wasn't going to help.

Mike leapt for the handhold above. His fingers grazed the lip of the hold.

He missed.

Mike fell. Below him, there were gasps and groans from the crowd, followed by more cheers for him to try again.

His second run was worse than his first.

The gap in The Monster had gotten into his head. It was all Mike could think about as he began his second climb.

He was only a short way up when his hand gave out entirely and the auto belay safely lowered him to the floor.

Two attempts failed. Only one left.

Mike shook out his hand and tried to forget about the pain. He wanted to give up and leave before he embarrassed himself again.

That was when he heard Annie's voice. "You can do it, big bro!"

Mike hurried over and knelt beside Annie.

"Hey, squirt," he said.

"Hey," she replied, casually adding, "Doing anything important right now?"

"Just humiliating myself in front of a bunch of people. No big," Mike said.

"You're not humiliating yourself," Annie said. "You're doing great."

"If I fall again, I'm done," he responded.

"Mike," Annie said, taking his hand. "You didn't come this far to only come this far."

He smiled. "Thanks, squirt."

Then he returned to The Monster, ready to conquer it once and for all.

CHAPTER 12

ONE LAST CLIMB

The third climb. It was now or never.

A new hush fell over the crowd. They knew what was at stake for Mike. He squeezed his left hand shut, felt pain lingering there. He had to fight through it, and he knew exactly how to do that.

He watched Annie do it every day of her life.

Mike slid both hands onto the first hold. He reached up with his right hand, grabbed the next thin hold, and drew his feet off the ground. Behind him, it was so quiet he heard the man in the tracksuit click his stopwatch.

The quiet was shattered.

"Stay focused, Mike! You can do it!" Hazel shouted. Others joined her with cheers of praise and encouragement.

Mike's arm muscles burned as he climbed. His hand was throbbing, but he ignored it. He just pictured the next hold and reached for it.

He was making good time. His heart raced. His hands sped across the wall. Before he knew it, he was past the spot where'd he fallen on his second run and was nearing the gap in the wall.

Don't overthink it, he reminded himself.

Mike reached the gap. He saw the hold above him, the one he'd missed so terribly before.

Mike tensed his legs and jumped.

He was airborne for a split second, but it felt like a lifetime. The fingers of his right hand touched the hold, slipped, then caught the lip.

He'd made it!

The crowd erupted. Mike pulled his left hand up to join his right and continued up the wall.

Mike scaled the rest of The Monster. At the top, another hold was boxed in with pink tape. Mike stretched and grabbed it with both hands.

"Course complete!" the judge yelled. He pressed the stopwatch and recorded Mike's time.

Mike looked down at Annie and waved.

He'd done it.

* * *

"Fourth place!" Hazel said. "In your very first competition. Not too shabby."

Hazel's words echoed through the silence of the Saturday morning haze. The sun was not up yet, the sky just a twinkling glow of dawn. She and Mike were walking along the top of the ridge, the one where he'd made his first climb. They weren't alone, though.

"He's already got a big enough head," Annie said. "No need to swell it any further."

"Quiet, you," Mike said as Hazel laughed.

Mike was pushing Annie's wheelchair along the bumpy ridge line. Their parents had found a pathway that led to the top of the cliff. They were still at the bottom getting the equipment and preparing for a morning of climbing.

It had been a week since Mike and Hazel had taken part in the King Crag Ultimate Indoor Competition. While Mike was proud of his fourth-place finish, he was also proud of his friend. "So," he asked Hazel, "how's it feel to beat Derek?"

Hazel, who'd won the competition, smiled. "Not gonna lie," she said. "Pretty amazing."

They continued to walk along the top of the cliff. It was slow going, but Mike didn't mind. Annie didn't seem to be bothered by the less than smooth ride she was getting, either. "Look at me," she said. "I'm off-roading."

When they reached the spot where they would climb, Mike and Hazel helped Annie out of her wheelchair. She could walk, just a bit, but Mike slipped her arm around his shoulder for support. "You good, squirt?" he asked.

"Yep," she answered.

The three of them walked to the cliff's edge, where Mike and Annie lowered themselves to the ground. They sat side by side, their feet dangling over the edge. Hazel sat on Annie's other side. They had a perfect view of the eastern horizon. Now, they just had to wait.

The trio sat in silence until the sun finally broke free of the mountain ridge. Sunlight lit up the crags and valleys before them. Birds circled high in the sky.

Mike finally broke the silence. "I can't believe I'm going to say this, but Principal Weathers was right."

Annie looked over at him. "About what?"

"About why we keep climbing," he said. "The view really is amazing."

ABOUT the AUTHOR

Brandon Terrell is the author of numerous children's books, working on such Capstone series as *Tony Hawk's 900 Revolution* and *Tony Hawk: Live2Skate*, *Spine Shivers*, *Michael Dahl Presents: Phobia*, *Sports Illustrated Kids: Time Machine Magazine*, *Jim Nasium and Snoops, Inc.* He has also written numerous sports stories for Capstone's Jake Maddox line of books and graphic novels. When not hunched over his laptop, Brandon enjoys watching movies and television, reading, watching and playing baseball, and spending time with his wife and two children at his home in Minnesota.

GLOSSARY

ascend (uh-SEND)—the process of moving upward

belayer (bi-LAY-ur)—a person who controls the safety rope while their partner is climbing

callus (KAL-uhss)—a hard, thickened area of skin

carabiner (KAYR-uh-BEE-nur)—a metal ring, usually shaped like a D, that is used in climbing to hold ropes

crag (KRAG)—a steep, sharp rock or cliff

crevasse (kri-VAS)—a deep, wide crack

descend (di-SEND)—to climb down

diagnosis (dye-uhg-noh-SISS)—the cause of a problem

harness (HAR-niss)—an arrangement of straps used to keep someone safe

muscular dystrophy (muhss-kyoo-LUR diss-troh-FEE)—a group of diseases that causes weakness and loss of muscle mass

piton (PEE-tahn)—a peg or spike that is driven into a rock for support

precipice (PRESS-uh-piss)—a steep cliff

DISCUSSION QUESTIONS

1. Do you think rock climbing has a positive effect on Mike's life? Use examples from the text to support your answer.

2. Why was it was important to Mike to climb The Monster during his first time at King Crag?

3. In what ways are Mike's and Hazel's families similar? In what ways are they different?

WRITING PROMPTS

1. Pretend you're Mike. Write a letter to your father after the day you hurt your hand.

2. Rewrite the scene in gym class from Vaughn's point of view. How does he feel about Mike? What is going through his mind when Mike tackles him?

3. Think about a time when you succeeded at a sport. Now write about that moment. How did you feel? What was going through your mind?

MORE ABOUT ROCK CLIMBING

Rock climbing developed as a sport in the 1800s. In 2020, sport climbers will compete in the Olympic games in Tokyo. This will be the first time the Olympics has a rock climbing event.

There are three different categories to competitive climbing: lead, bouldering, and speed. Lead climbing challenges climbers to get as high as they can on routes as high as 60 feet (18 meters). Competitors climb for time in speed climbing, while bouldering measure routes, attempts, and special bonus holds.

Devils Tower, a national monument in Wyoming, is a popular rock climbing site. The tower is 865 feet (264 m) high. In 2018, 87-year-old Robert Kelman became the oldest person to successfully climb it.